W9-BJC-046

AARON M. WASOWSKI
5125 Rowantree Place, South Bend, IN 46619

A NOTE TO PARENTS

When your children are ready to "step into reading," giving them the right books—and lots of them—is as crucial as giving them the right food to eat. **Step into Reading Books** present exciting stories and information reinforced with lively, colorful illustrations that make learning to read fun, satisfying, and worthwhile. They are priced so that acquiring an entire library of them is affordable. And they are beginning readers with an important difference—they're written on four levels.

Step 1 Books, with their very large type and extremely simple vocabulary, have been created for the very youngest readers. **Step 2 Books** are both longer and slightly more difficult. **Step 3 Books,** written to mid-second-grade reading levels, are for the child who has acquired even greater reading skills. **Step 4 Books** offer exciting nonfiction for the increasingly proficient reader.

Children develop at different ages. **Step into Reading Books,** with their four levels of reading, are designed to help children become good—and interested—readers *faster.* The grade levels assigned to the four steps—preschool through grade 1 for Step 1, grades 1 through 3 for Step 2, grades 2 and 3 for Step 3, and grades 2 through 4 for Step 4—are intended only as guides. Some children move through all four steps very rapidly; others climb the steps over a period of several years. These books will help your child "step into reading" in style!

Library of Congress Cataloging-in-Publication Data: Haus, Felice. Happy birthday, Cookie
Monster! (Step into reading. A Step 1 book) "Featuring Jim Henson's Sesame Street Muppets."
SUMMARY: Unable to help himself, Cookie Monster eats the cake he'd baked for his birthday
party, but his friends come through with appropriate presents so all the guests can be fed.
[1. Cake—Fiction. 2. Puppets—Fiction. 3. Birthdays—Fiction] I. Nicklaus, Carol, ill.
II. Children's Television Workshop. III. Sesame Street (Television program) IV. Title.
V. Series. PZ7.H2879Hap 1986 [E] 85-25639 ISBN: 0-394-88182-6 (trade);
0-394-98182-0 (lib. bdg.)

Manufactured in the United States of America   9 0

Step into Reading

Happy Birthday, Cookie Monster!

Featuring Jim Henson's Sesame Street Muppets

by Felice Haus

illustrated by Carol Nicklaus

A Step 1 Book

Random House / Children's Television Workshop

Who is this?

It looks

like Cookie Monster.

It talks

like Cookie Monster.

Crunch, crunch,
gobble and gulp.
It eats
like Cookie Monster.

Yes, it is Cookie Monster.

Hello, Cookie!

What is Cookie doing?

Is he baking cookies?

Is he baking a pie?

No, Cookie is baking
a cake.

Today is his birthday!
He is having a party.

Is it a good cake?
Yes, it is good!
His friends will like it.

It is very, very good!

Why is Cookie sad?

He has eaten
all the cake.
Now he has no cake
for his party.

Ding, dong!

Who is at the door?

It is Big Bird.
He gives Cookie
a present.

Ding, dong!
It is Grover
with a present
for Cookie.

Ding, dong!
It is Ernie and Bert.
They have a present
for Cookie too.

But Cookie has
no birthday cake
for them.

His friends say,
"Do not be sad, Cookie.
Open your presents."

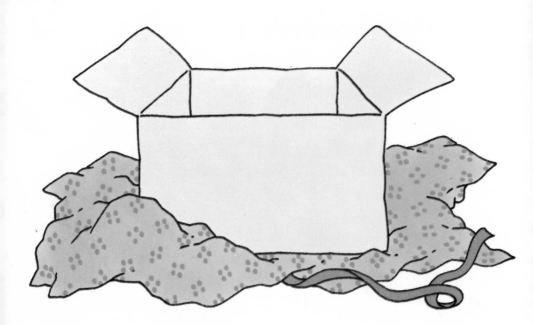

Inside Big Bird's box

is a yellow cake!

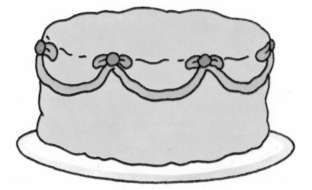

Cookie gives everyone
a piece.

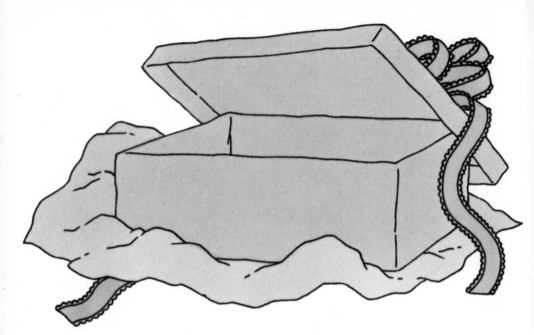

Inside Grover's box

is a blue cake!

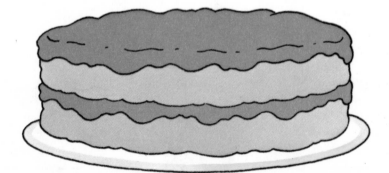

Cookie gives everyone
a piece.

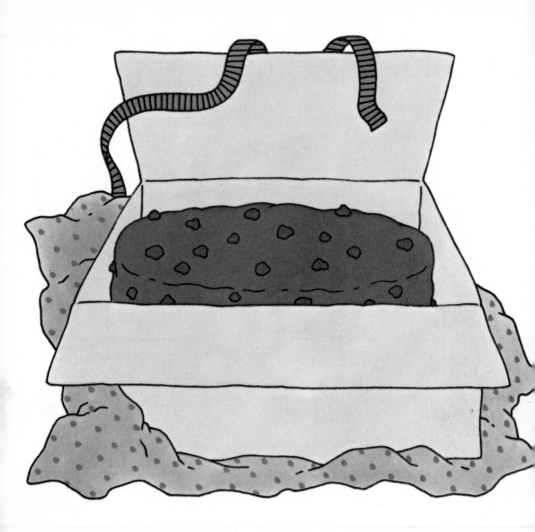

Inside Ernie and Bert's box is a chocolate chip cookie cake!

Cookie gives everyone
a piece.

Inside everyone is
lots and lots of cake!

Now Cookie is
very happy.

Happy birthday,
Cookie Monster.